PLAYDATE PALS

Hippo is HAPPY

Rosie Greening • Dawn Machell

make believe ideas

One day Puppy saw **Hippo** looking **sad**, so he gave her an empty book with a big **smiley** face on it.

“Why don’t you fill it with things that make you **happy**?” suggested Puppy. **Hippo** opened the book and started to think.

First **Hippo** thought about **playing** in the park.

That made her **happy**!

Next, **Hippo** thought about **jumping** in puddles.

"I **love** splashing around with
my friends!" she thought.

Then **Hippo** thought about **playing** with her favorite toys – that made her **happy**, too!

Hippo imagined **eating** ice cream, and her tummy gave a rumble.

“Ice cream makes me **really happy**!” **giggled** Hippo.

After that **Hippo** thought
about getting a big **hug**.

“**Hugs** always make me **happy**.
And I **love** giving them, too!” she thought.

Finally **Hippo** thought about falling **asleep** in her bed.

"I feel **happy** and **safe** when I'm in bed," thought **Hippo**.

Hippo had lots of ideas, so Puppy offered to help her put them in the book.

They had lots of **fun**
drawing together, and
that made **Hippo happy**, too!

When the book was full, **Hippo** added stickers to make them look extra special.

“**Hooray**! My book is finished!” said **Hippo**, and she **jumped** with **excitement**.

Hippo and Puppy looked through the book together. "What a lovely book!" said Puppy.

Hippo felt a warm, **tingly** feeling in her tummy, and she gave a big **smile**.

Being **friends** with Puppy
made her **happiest** of all!

READING TOGETHER

Playdate Pals have been written for parents, caregivers, and teachers to share with young children who are beginning to explore the feelings they have about themselves and the world around them.

Each story is intended as a springboard to emotional discovery and can be used to gently promote further discussion around the feeling or behavioral topic featured in the book.

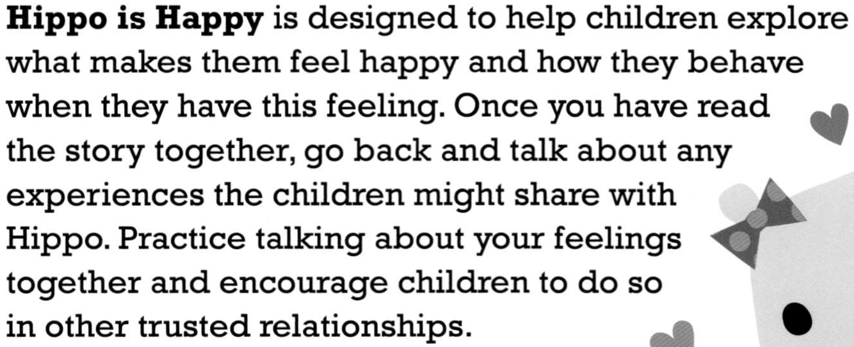

Hippo is Happy is designed to help children explore what makes them feel happy and how they behave when they have this feeling. Once you have read the story together, go back and talk about any experiences the children might share with Hippo. Practice talking about your feelings together and encourage children to do so in other trusted relationships.

Look at the pictures

Talk about the characters. Are they smiling, laughing, hugging each other, or jumping up and down? Help children think about what people look like or how they move their bodies when they are happy.

Words in bold

Throughout each story there are words highlighted in bold type. These words specify either the **character's name** or useful words and phrases relating to feeling **happy**. You may wish to put emphasis on these words or use them as reminders for parts of the story you can return to and discuss.

Questions you can ask

To prompt further exploration of this feeling, you could try asking children some of the following questions:

- What makes you feel happy and how do you show it?
- When you are happy, what does it feel like in your body?
- What can you do to make other people feel happy?
- Can you make a happy face?